THE SNAIL HOUSE

For Solly
G.T.
And Kate
A.A.

First published 2000 by Walker Books Ltd
87 Vauxhall Walk, London SE11 5HJ

10 9 8 7 6 5 4 3 2 1

Text © 2000 Allan Ahlberg
Illustrations © 2000 Gillian Tyler

This book has been typeset in Golden Cockerel.

Printed in Hong Kong

British Library Cataloguing in Publication Data
A catalogue record for this book
is available from the British Library.

ISBN 0-7445-6164-7

ALLAN AHLBERG
THE SNAIL HOUSE

Illustrated by

GILLIAN TYLER

WALKER BOOKS
AND SUBSIDIARIES
LONDON • BOSTON • SYDNEY

"Come here, children," Grandma said.
The children came.

"Gather round – climb up now."

And so they did, all warm and sweetly-smelling from their strawberry picking, and into Grandma's lap.

"A story, Grandma?" Michael said.

"Story?" added Hannah.

"A story … yes," said Grandma.

"About the horses?" Michael said.

"Hozzes?" added Hannah.

"No – no hozzes this time, sweetheart." Grandma cuddled them up inside her mighty arms. "This time," – she gazed across the dusty evening garden – "this time it's the turn … of something else."

"Once upon a long long time ago there was a boy and his sister and their little baby brother who all of a sudden got so very very small that they could leave that house of theirs by a crack under the door – and *no one notice.*"

"My!" said Hannah.

"So one day that's just exactly what they did. They left that house, all on a bright and sunny morning, the dew still on the grass, and went to live, for a little while at least, in their own, their absolutely very own and private … snail house."

"Snail house?" cried Michael.

"Snail house – yes."

"On the back of a snail?"

"That's right. And it was a proper house too, with a door and windows, roof and chimney, table, chairs, three little beds, curtains and crockery – everything!"

"It have a TV?" Hannah said.

"No TV, sweetheart, not in those days. But a radio, yes."

"So there they lived in that house, which of course was a *moving* house. And they kept it spotless clean; dusting the furniture, sweeping the floor, washing the windows. And they fed that snail friend of theirs as well, with bits of lettuce and such. And they read books, hung their washing on the line, minded the baby…"

"And had *adventures*," Michael said.

"And had adventures," Grandma said. "Three adventures, actually."

"One each," said Michael.

"Hm, sort of." Grandma leant across to the baby in his pushchair. His little cotton sunhat had slid down over his sleeping face. She moved the hat aside.

"The first adventure that those children had was … the *earthquake*. One minute they were having breakfast, the baby in his highchair, the sun shining, grasshoppers chirruping, radio on. Then, all of a sudden – wallop! – the whole snail house shook. Plates smashed, chairs fell over and that poor old snail himself just wobbled like a jelly."

"It was a human being, I'll bet!" cried Michael. "Stamping around."

"Or pussycat," added Hannah.

"No – no person caused that sudden thump, nor pussycat neither. No, you'll just about never guess." Grandma waved a flitting moth away. "You see, what caused that earthquake was … an *apple*."

"Falling from a tree!" cried Michael.

"That's right. Bouncing down upon that orchard grass like a bomb, and missing the snail by inches."

"Then did they eat it?" Hannah asked.

"Well, some of it. It was pretty big for them, you see. Only then they shared it, sort of, with a young red fox who just that very moment came slipping through those orchard trees towards the river."

"After the ducks," said Michael.

"Hm." Grandma shuffled her load of children and made herself more comfortable on the wide verandah steps. Traffic hummed on the distant road, headlights faintly gleaming in the gathering dark.

"The second adventure that those children had was … the *disappearing baby*. He just crawled off one time, while his brother and sister were playing catch – for only a moment, it seemed – and was lost from sight in the forest of grass. Well, those children, once they realized what had happened, looked everywhere for that infant, ever more frantic and tearful too, till – lo and behold – they spotted him."

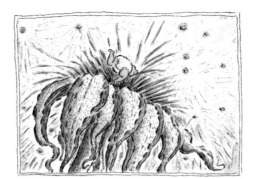

"Ah!" said Hannah.

"Yes, spotted him … halfway up a dandelion stalk. See, it was leaning over, not growing straight. *Next* thing, he was floating away, that baby, hanging on tight to one of those fluffy seeds."

"Like a parachute!" cried Michael.

"Hm … floating away … and floating." Grandma paused. Next door a phone was ringing.

"They catch him?" Hannah asked.

"By and by, oh yes, after much puffing and running and chasing, they caught him and carried him home."

"To the snail house," Michael said.

"The snail house," Grandma said.

"The third adventure, though, was the
scary one." That phone again, and now
a dog barking. "This began one evening
right after a shower of rain, the drops
like sacks of water exploding all around.
The snail house was moving through the
half-light and the dampness – conditions
which a snail most loves – when …
there was a heavy movement above …
a shadow."

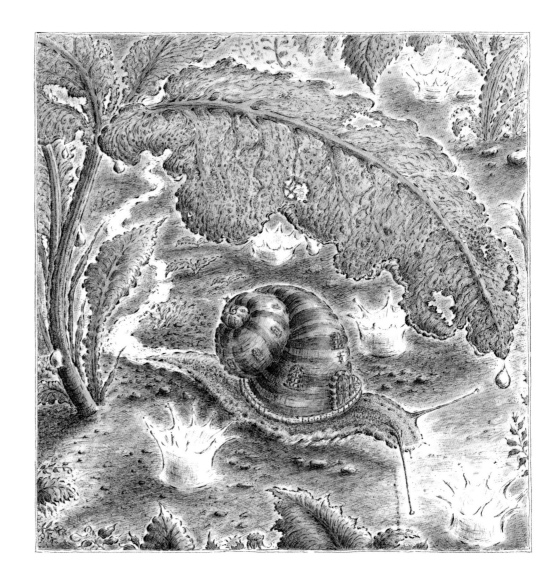

"The children felt it in their house and peeped out of the window."

"What they see?" said Hannah.

"I know," said Michael.

"They see … they saw, high above and all before them, advancing stately through the grass – a mighty giant bird."

"Oh!" cried Hannah.

"It was a thrush – a lovely singing bird, of course, but for a snail, you see —"

"Thrushes eat snails!" cried Michael.

"That's right. For a snail, I'm bound to say, a thrush was a *tiger* in that garden. And on it came on its beanpole legs, looking here and there with its dark eye—"

"They smash their shells on a rock!" cried Michael.

"No!" cried Hannah.

"Well, that poor old snail just tucked his head in and hoped. But the children, though, they grabbed some pots and pans and rushed outside, banging and clattering and hollering—"

"Scared it off!" cried Hannah.

"No, sweetie, not quite, though they were hugely brave to try. No, it was a sudden prowling cat did that. She was the tiger in the thrush's garden. Hm."

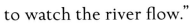

Just then another
actual cat came
brushing against them
in the darkness on the verandah.
  "Then up that thrush went flying
into a tall tree, and off that cat went
prowling some more—"
  "Here's *your* cat, Grandma,"
Michael said.
  "Monty, Monty," Hannah called.
  "And, by and by, off and away on its
ever-shiny trail went the snail house,
under the brightening stars,
down at last, come midnight,
to the very water's edge …
      to watch the river flow."

The pushchair squeaked. The baby was stirring, his pale round face like a luminous clock in the dark.

"Which is the end," said Grandma, planting the children on the steps and rising to her feet.

"Next day, having properly thanked that snail for his house and hospitality, they went back to their proper size … and home."

In the kitchen Michael put on the light. Grandma – the slowly-waking baby now in her arms – came following after. Out on the verandah Hannah was standing yet, gazing into the muffled blackness of the garden.

The cat was sitting on the top verandah step, while over and beyond the invisible hedge horses were whinnying.